ISBN 978-1-338-86256-0

10 9 8 7 6 5 4 3 2 1          23 24 25 26 27

Printed in Malaysia    106

First edition 2023

Book design by Jessica Rodriguez
Stock photos © Shutterstock.com

# FOIL WONDERS!
## PEEL, STICK, AND DECORATE!

In your hands is a very special book. By using the foil paper, you'll be able to decorate scenes and images with shiny colors.

**1**

Select the color of foil paper that you'd like to use. Set aside.

**2**

In the pages of the book, carefully peel the area that you'd like to color with foil. (Note: It should already be perforated.) Discard the peeled top.

**3**

Pick up the foil paper you set aside in step 1. With the color side facing you, press the foil paper into the area of the page that you just peeled. You should see the outline of the shape that you're decorating through the foil sheet.

Tip: Use a toothpick to remove very small sticker areas. Then, use the same toothpick to gently apply the foil to the sticker.

**4**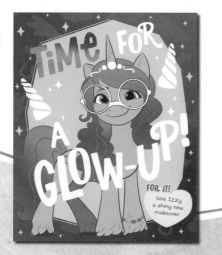

Slowly peel the sheet of foil away. Ta-da! Admire your creation.

Tip: Once you've used a section of foil, it cannot be reused. We recommend starting with a corner of the sheet when decorating to maximize your foil paper.

# CHANGE IS IN THE AIR!

This book contains three stories about change. Read along and watch as the ponies and their world are transformed!

# BESTiES

**FOiL iT!**

Glow up this pic of Sunny and her friends.

# CHANGE STARTS AT HOME

Sunny, Hitch, and Sprout were playing with their pony toys.

"My mom says the Pegasi and Unicorns are
our enemies," Sprout said, holding up a Unicorn toy.
"They'll zap us with lasers."

"That's a lie!" Sunny exclaimed.
"They wouldn't do that."

"Well, that is kinda what our teacher
said in history class," Hitch said.

But Sunny didn't believe it. She just knew that the Pegasi
and Unicorns could be friends with the Earth Ponies.

"What's the matter, Sunny?" asked Sunny's father, Argyle, after Hitch and Sprout left.

"They still don't believe me about the Unicorns and Pegasi," Sunny replied sadly.

"The important thing is that you stand up for what you believe in," Argyle said with a smile.

"Someday both of us will meet Unicorns, or a Pegasus, and we'll be best friends forever," Sunny said.

"Well, maybe today is that day," Argyle replied. "Look! A Unicorn!"

"Where?" Sunny gasped.

"Over here," laughed Argyle. He was wearing a paper Unicorn horn. What a fun transformation!

Later, Argyle helped Sunny write a letter.

"Dear Unicorns and Pegasi, you have friends in Maretime Bay. Come visit us!" it said.

They attached the letter to a floating lantern and sent it soaring into the distance.

**FOiL iT!**
Help Sunny send her message to the Unicorns and Pegasi.

LeT'S SHiNe TOGeTHeR

That night, Argyle had a special surprise for Sunny: a carousel he had made that celebrated all types of ponies together.

"Wow! You finished it!" Sunny exclaimed.

"Pretty neat, huh?" Argyle answered. He turned the carousel on. Bright images of Earth Ponies, Unicorns, and Pegasi filled the room.

"It's beautiful," Sunny said sleepily. She gazed around her transformed room, dreaming happily of the day all ponies could live in harmony.

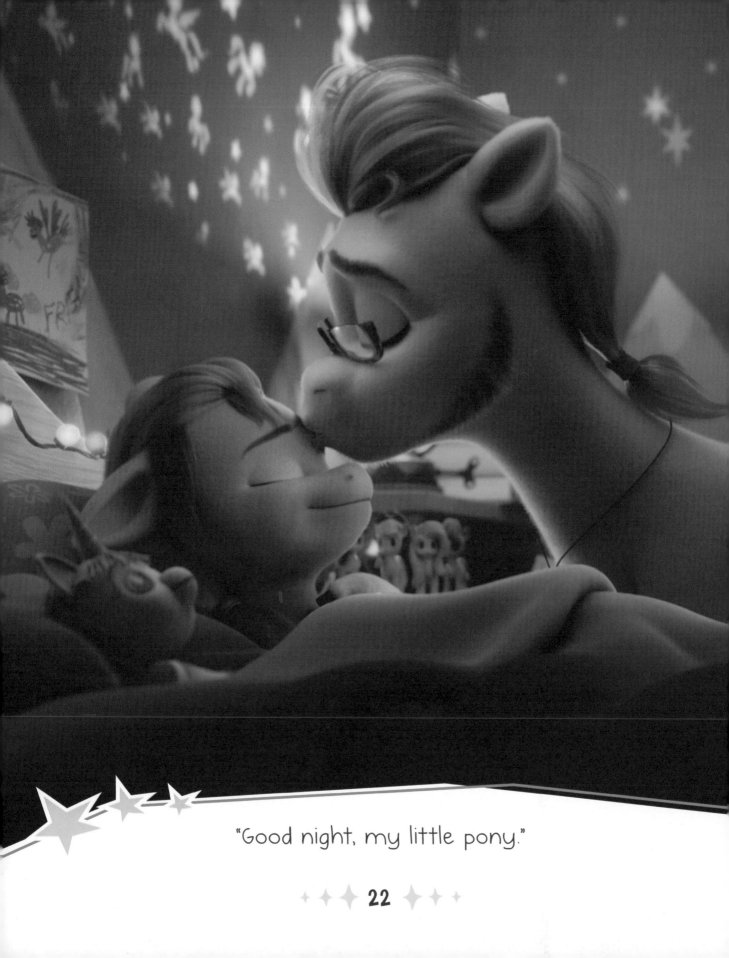

"Good night, my little pony."

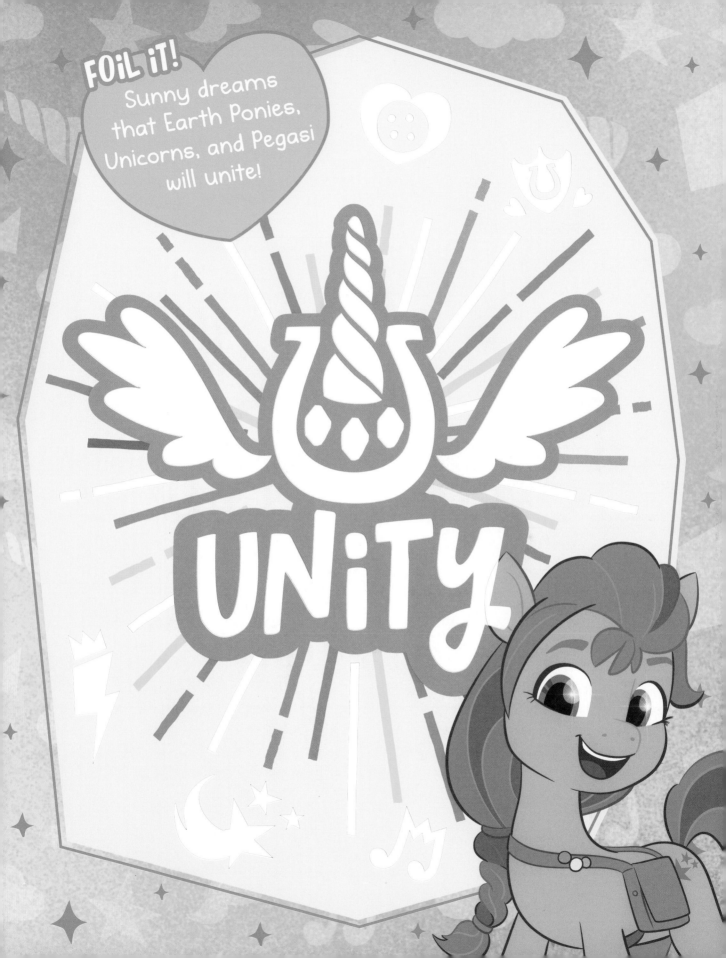

# PONY MAKEOVER

Sunny, Izzy, Pipp, Zipp, and Hitch had been traveling all day to get from Zephyr Heights, the home of the Pegasi, to Bridlewood, the home of the Unicorns.
They had finally arrived.

"Come on! My house isn't far from here," Izzy exclaimed.

Izzy's friends felt nervous as they walked through the woods.

"We're going to stick out like sore hooves," Sunny said anxiously. "We need to look like Unicorns."

"We need makeovers," Sunny said when they arrived at Izzy's house. "So, Izzy, can you do it?"

"A glow-up?" said Izzy. She smiled and grabbed her hair dryer. "Honey, you came to the right cottage."

Hitch was a little nervous, but the other ponies were excited.

"Yay, makeovers! I love makeovers," sighed Pipp.

"Don't worry, Hitch. You're in good hooves," Izzy reassured her friend.

TIME FOR A GLOW-UP!

FOIL IT!

Give Izzy a shiny new makeover.

Izzy whipped out a ruler and
measured Zipp's mane.

"Mm-hmm, mm-hmm," she said
with a nod. "I know just what to do.
You're gonna fit right in!"

Izzy rushed around her home gathering everything she would need for a fabulous pony makeover. She grabbed scissors, paper, paint, and a paintbrush.

"Unicorn horns for everypony!" she cried.

Izzy worked fast. When she was done, all the ponies sported glittery, multicolored horns on their foreheads.

"Thanks, Izzy!" Sunny said. "You're
right—we *do* fit right in."

"You're looking Unicorn strong," Izzy giggled. "What a transformation. Now let's get out there and change the world!"

# UNITED AT LAST

It had been hard work finding the magical crystals that Sunny hoped would reunite all ponies, but they had finally done it.

"It's time to put the crystals together, everypony," Sunny announced.

Sunny and Izzy carefully slid two of
the crystals together, but nothing happened.

Sunny thought for a moment.

"Oh, wait!" she said. "There's another
crystal in my special carousel. I bet that
one goes in the middle."

Sunny grabbed the third crystal and
placed it in the center, completing the design.
But still nothing happened.

"It . . . it didn't work," Izzy said.

"But why?" Sunny wondered.

"I think I understand," Sunny said slowly. "It's not the crystals that need to be brought together. It's us. We can choose friendship. That's the true magic."

Alphabittle, Phyllis, and Queen Haven, who were standing nearby, all nodded. One by one, they pushed together the pieces of a broken picture of Sunny and her father.

The ground began to shake. One crystal began to glow and float upward. The other two crystals quickly followed.

"What?" Sunny gasped as the floating crystals began to swirl around her, moving faster and faster. Her hooves lifted off the ground.

"Oh!" cried Izzy, Pipp, Zipp, and Hitch as their friend rose into the air.

Everypony watched in astonishment
as Sunny sprouted two glowing wings and a
glowing horn. She had become an Alicorn!

The moment Sunny's
transformation was complete,
a magical explosion
rocked the world.

"Whoa," Izzy exclaimed, delighted,
as her horn began to glow.

"We're actually flying!" screeched
Pipp and Zipp, flapping their wings as they
bounded through the air.

The magic was back!

We ARE the FUTURE!

FOiL iT!
Help Sunny and her friends celebrate the magic.

"You did it, Sunny," Hitch said as all
of Sunny's friends gathered around her.

"No. We all did it," Sunny replied.
"Besties forever—let's shine together!"

Use the foil sheets to give the images in this book a sparkly makeover.

# SMiLe, SPARKLe, SHiNe!